the magic
fairy ...

Gwyneth Rees is half Welsh and half English and grew up in Scotland. She went to Glasgow University and qualified as a doctor in 1990. She is a child and adolescent psychiatrist, but has now stopped practising so she can write full-time. Gwyneth is the author of the bestselling Fairies series – *Fairy Dust*, *Fairy Treasure*, *Fairy Dreams* and *Fairy Gold* – as well as *Mermaid Magic* and *Cosmo and the Magic Sneeze*. For older readers she has written *My Mum's from Planet Pluto*, *The Making of May*, *The Mum Hunt* (which won the Younger Novel category of the Red House Children's Book Award 2004) and its sequel, *The Mum Detective*. She lives in London with her two cats.

Visit www.gwynethrees.com

Amanda Li is a writer and editor who has worked in children's publishing for many years. She lives in London with her family.

Gwyneth Rees

the magical book of fairy fun

Compiled by Amanda Li

Illustrated by Emily Bannister

MACMILLAN CHILDREN'S BOOKS

First published 2006 by Macmillan Children's Books
a division of Macmillan Publishers Limited
20 New Wharf Road, London N1 9RR
Basingstoke and Oxford
www.panmacmillan.com

Associated companies throughout the world

ISBN-13: 978-0-330-44421-7
ISBN-10: 0-330-44421-2

1 3 5 7 9 8 6 4 2

A CIP catalogue record for this book is available from
the British Library.

Typeset by Nigel Hazle
Printed and bound in Great Britain by Mackays of Chatham plc, Kent

Contents

Cast of Fairies

Ruby

Snowdrop

Queen Amethys

Queen Mae

Queen Celeste

Goldie

Bonnie

Sapphire

Cammie the
wee man

Emerald

Moonbeam

Buttercup

Star

1

From Gwyneth Rees

If you're a fairy fan then I'm sure you'll love my
Magical Book of Fairy Fun! It has all my favourite
fairies in it – Snowdrop, Ruby, Emerald,
Sapphire, Star, Moonbeam, Goldie, Bonnie,
Precious and Cammie (the wee man). There are
lots of puzzles and quizzes in this book and
they've all been made especially for children who
love fairies.

I've written about four types of fairies in my
books – flower fairies in *Fairy Dust*, book fairies
in *Fairy Treasure*, dream fairies in *Fairy Dreams*
and tooth fairies in *Fairy Gold*. I don't know
which kind of fairy I'd most like to be, but maybe
I'd be a book fairy since I like books so much!

Sometimes children write and ask me if I've ever
seen a *real* fairy. The answer to that is that I *have*
seen fairies, but I'm not sure if they were real
ones or not. It happened when I was about eight
years old. I was lying in bed because I was sick

with a really high temperature. My bed faced the window and when I looked across at my curtains I suddenly saw lots of little fairies dancing across the top of them. They were gold and sparkly and very tiny and I thought they looked a bit like Tinkerbell, the fairy in the story of *Peter Pan*. I was very excited and I called out to my mum to tell her about them. When my mum came into my room she couldn't see the fairies and she said I must be just imagining them because I had a fever. The fairies went away and I never saw them again after that.

Maybe my mum was right and my mind was just playing tricks on me because I was so ill! Or maybe not! What do *you* think?

In my books, I often write about things that have happened to me in real life – like seeing fairies when I was sick – but I also enjoy making my characters do things that I've never actually done myself but would really *love* to do if I got the chance! For instance, I'd really love to go to a fairy party, so that's why there are so many fairy

4

parties in my books. I think that getting to dress up like a fairy and eat all that gorgeous fairy food would be brilliant fun!

I hope you agree with me that fairies *are* fun – and if you do then I'm sure you'll find lots of fun things to do inside this book!

Odd One Out 1

Shh! Don't disturb the fairies. They're gathered together for one of their fairy parties.

Look very carefully and see if you can find four fairies who are different from the rest.

Circle the four fairies.

1 2 3

4 5 6

7 8 9

10 11 12

13 14 15

The answers are on page 143.

Dolphin Dilemma

Rosie must find her way to the magical fairy island.

Which dolphin trail will lead her boat there?

A

C

B

8

The answer is on page 143.

Fairy Crossword

CLUES

Across

1. Fairies use these to fly with.
2. She's the royal head of the fairies.
3. You might see tiny specks of this floating around when the fairies are making magic.
5. A place that all book fairies love.
6. Fairies just love to eat this.

Down

1. Every fairy needs to wave one of these.
4. Fairy jewels shine and . . .

The answers are on page 143.

Fairy Clothes Match

Can you draw a line between each garment and its exact double?

Which piece of clothing has no double?

The answer is on page 143.

Colour Queen Mae

In *Fairy Dust*, Rosie is lucky enough to meet the beautiful Queen Mae. Read the queen's description below and colour the picture.

'At the back of the courtyard was a very beautiful fairy, sitting on a tree trunk throne that was scattered with gold rose petals. She was wearing a cream silk petticoat with an outer skirt of deep-pink petals and her bodice was made of woven lavender. Her large wings were spread open behind her, glittering in the moonlight. On top of her wavy, golden hair she wore a purple floral crown.'

Fairy Tip: Use the brightest yellow you can find for her golden hair and the gold rose petals.

Magical Mix-up

The fairies have mixed up some words that describe them.

Can you unscramble the letters and write the words in the spaces?

n *d*
i *k*

y *n*
i *t*

1. _ _ _ _

2. _ _ _ _ _

l p l f

u e h

3. _ _ _ _ _ _

y t t

e r p

4. _ _ _ _ _ _

s w

e t e

5. _ _ _ _ _

The answers are on page 143.

11

Birthday Baking

The fairies have baked you a special cake for your birthday!

Write your age in the middle of the cake and draw the right number of candles. Buttercup has put one on already.

Dotty Drawing 1

Colour in the shapes that have a dot in them to find one of the fairies' favourite creatures.

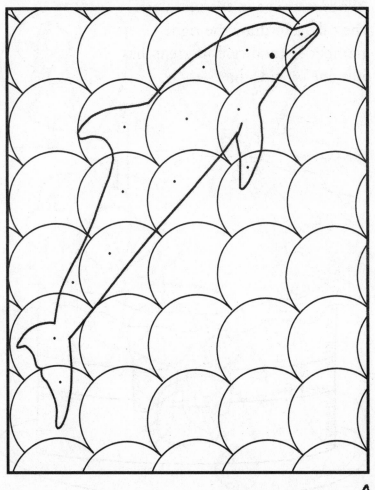

Find Cammie's Sock

Cammie MacPherson has lost his tartan sock. Can you help him find it by tracing the right piece of wool?

The answer is on page 143.

20

Fairy Favourites

Can you unscramble the words to find six of the fairies' favourite things?

1. ELOCATHOC   _ _ _ _ _ _ _ _ _

2. ADNWS   _ _ _ _ _

3. CNIPSIC   _ _ _ _ _ _ _

4. SCIMU   _ _ _ _ _

5. HESOS   _ _ _ _ _

6. EPISTAR   _ _ _ _ _ _ _

The answers are on page 144.

Copy and Colour 1

Copy this picture of Connie, from *Fairy Treasure*, square by square. Then colour her in.

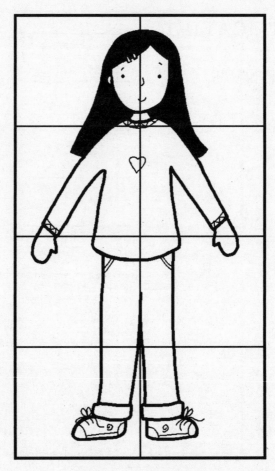

Puzzling Piles

Ruby the book fairy needs to get all her books on to the library shelves.

It's a big job so she wants to start with the largest pile.

Which pile has the most books? Write the numbers in the boxes below.

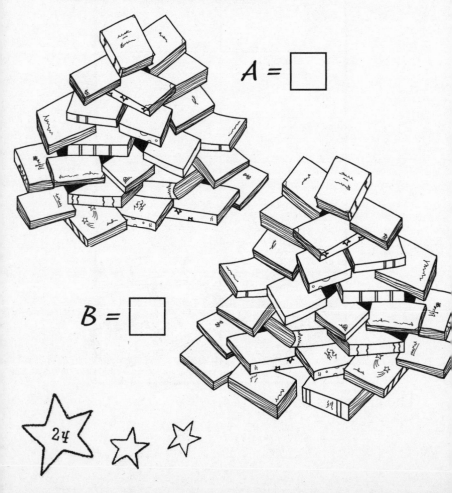

$A = \boxed{}$

$B = \boxed{}$

24

$C = \boxed{}$

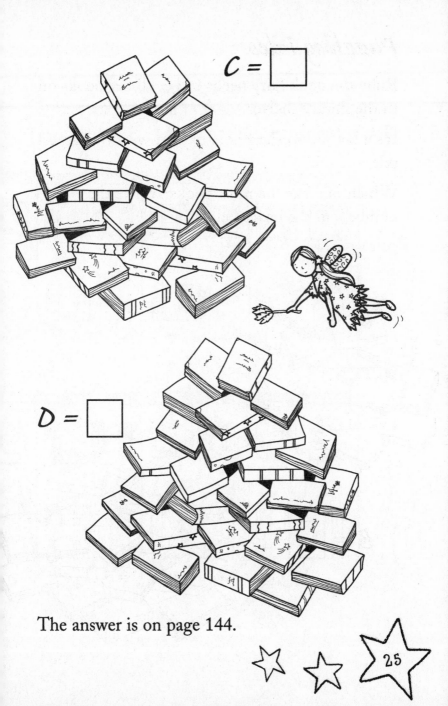

$D = \boxed{}$

The answer is on page 144.

25

Find the Fairies

The book fairies are feeling a bit shy today, so they're hiding in this street of entry books. How many fairies can you find?

The answers are on page 144.

27

Biscuit Blunder

Whoops! One of the book fairies has dropped her letter biscuits on the way to the fairy picnic.

The biscuits spell out three fairy names. They are also the names of three precious stones. Can you write the names in the spaces below? We've done the first three letters already.

1. _E_ _ _ _ _ _ _

2. _R_ _ _ _ _

3. _S_ _ _ _ _ _ _ _

28

Fairy Tip

Cross out the biscuits as you use each letter.

The answers are on page 144.

29

Pick the Page

The fairy librarian looks after all the library books very carefully, using special magic water to wash the pages. Can you match these dry pages back to the right books for her?

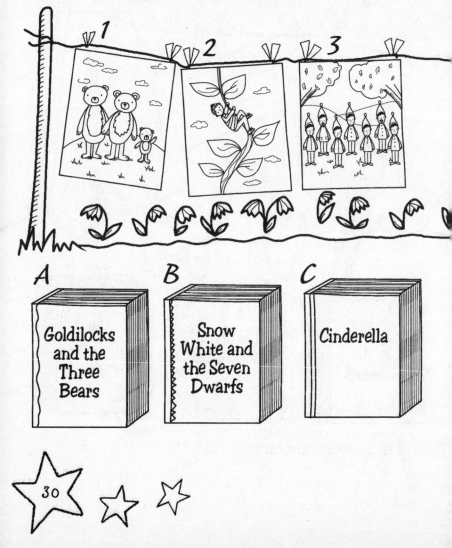

A **Goldilocks and the Three Bears**

B **Snow White and the Seven Dwarfs**

C **Cinderella**

D

Jack
and the
Beanstalk

E

Aladdin

F

The
Gingerbread
Man

The answers are on page 144.

Copy and Colour 2

Copy the picture of Ruby square by square. Then colour her in.

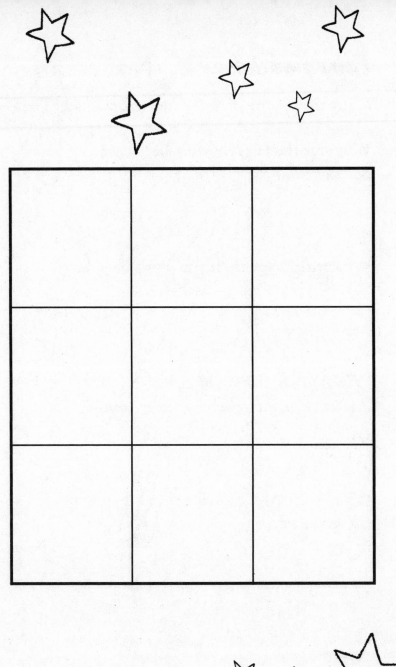

33

Fairy Fun 1

Why was the fairy blowing her nose?
She was having a cold spell.

What would you do if you saw a blue fairy?
Try to cheer her up.

Why do fairies sit on toadstools?
Because there isn't mushroom in the woods.

What is it that fairies like about dolphins?
Oh, lots of fins.

Dot to Dot 1

Join the letters of the alphabet to find something growing in the fairy forest.

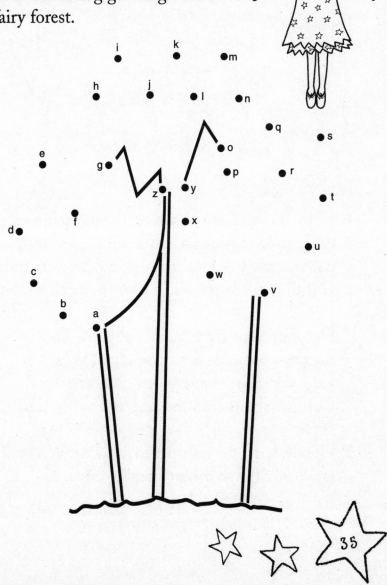

Make a Fairy Door Hanger

Why not make a fabulous fairy door hanger to hang outside your bedroom?

It's easy!

You will need:

A piece of thin white card
Scissors
Coloured pens to decorate

How to make

1. Copy the shape opposite on to your piece of card, or trace it on to a piece of paper, cut it out and use this as a template to draw around.
2. Cut the card shape out. Draw the circle at the top.
3. Decorate your hanger and colour it. Look at the page opposite for a few ideas. Why not write different messages on each side?
4. Cut through the dotted line and cut out the circle.
5. Finally, hang on your bedroom door. Why not make one for your best friend too?

Fairies about –
KEEP OUT!

Flower Wordsnake

Trace out the fairies' favourite flowers in the grid opposite. The words below go in one continuous line, snaking up and down, backwards and forwards, but never diagonally.

Use a pencil to trace the snake.

BLUEBELL
ROSE
DAFFODIL
DAISY
BUTTERCUP
SNOWDROP
LILY
HONEYSUCKLE
TULIP
PRIMROSE

B	L	U	E	D	A	F
E	B	E	S	D	O	F
L	L	R	O	I	L	D
E	S	O	R	M	I	A
U	L	I	P	P	R	I
T	E	L	U	B	Y	S
U	C	K	T	T	E	R
S	Y	E	S	P	U	C
H	O	N	N	O	W	D
Y	L	I	L	P	O	R

The answer is on page 145.

39

Dotty Drawing 2

Colour in the shapes that have a dot in them to find one of the fairies' favourite creatures.

Odd One Out 2

One of these bunches of flowers is different from the others.

Can you find it?

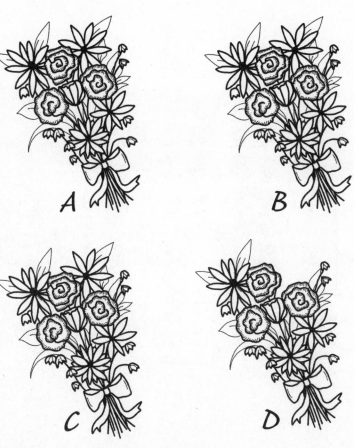

A

B

C

D

The answer is on page 145.

Puzzling Palaces

Evie and the fairies Star and Moonbeam are visiting Queen Celeste's palace. Can you find six differences between the two pictures?

The answers are on page 145.

Where's the Wand?

Oh dear! This little fairy has lost her wand.
Can you help her find a way through the maze to
reach it?

The answer is on page 146.

Draw the Missing Half

Can you complete this picture of Evie?
Then colour the picture in.

Party Shopping

The fairies are planning a party. Can you help them with their shopping?

Fill in the missing letters to find out what's on their list.

1. _NVIT_T_ONS
2. L_MO_ADE
3. __SCUITS
4. S_R_WS
5. C_O__LA_E MU_FI_S
6. CR__PS

The answers are on page 146.

Colouring Fun 1

Using the colour guide below, can you colour in this picture of Evie and Queen Celeste?

1. Blue
2. Yellow
3. Brown
4. Pink

Match the Shoes

Twinkle the fairy has been busy with her magic shoe dust, creating lots of lovely pairs of shoes for her fairy friends.

There are so many of them, they've got mixed up.

Can you help her by drawing a pencil line between the matching pairs?

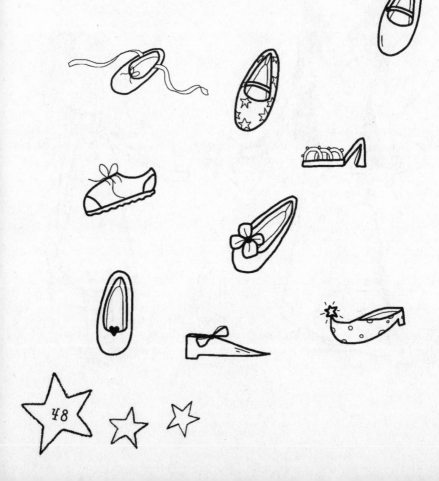

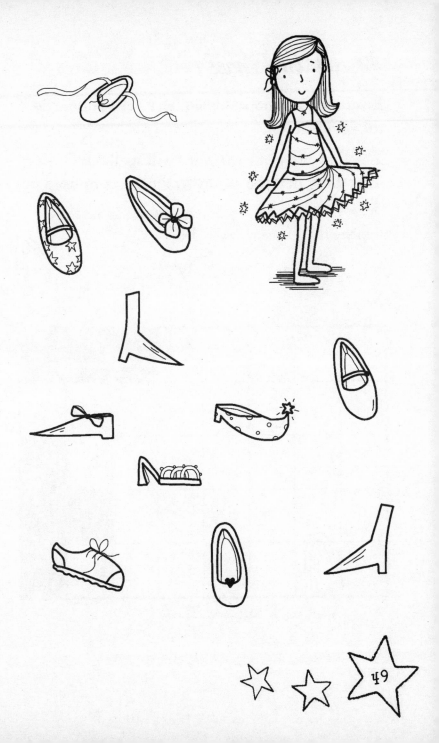

Fairy Word Grid 1

Read the clues opposite and write the answers in the grid below.

The first letter of each word will spell out something that the fairies like to make dresses out of.

Clues

1. Fairies love music and dancing. They always look forward to a fairy ....

2. When a fairy has written a letter she puts it into a fairy ....

3. Fairy lights and stars do this. It's also the first word of a famous song about a little star.

4. Fairies like eating all kinds of fruit: berries and bananas, oranges and ....

5. Fairies sometimes use this kind of lamp to light up a night-time party.

The answers are on page 146.

Design a Party Outfit

Wow! The fairies have invited you to a fantastic fairy party.

Can you create a beautiful dress to wear and draw it on the figure opposite?

Add some shoes, a new bag and some super hair decorations, using our ideas below.

Then all you have to do is get ready to shrink!

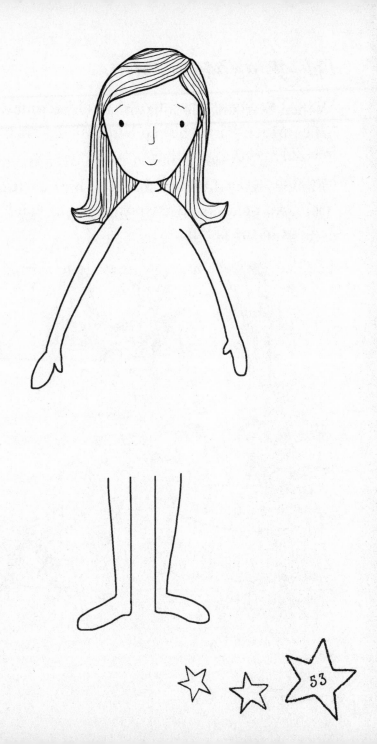

The Blue Moon Party

When Star and Moonbeam take Evie to the Blue Moon Party she can hardly believe her eyes. Everything is blue!

Find as many different shades of blue felt-tips, coloured pencils and crayons as you can and colour in the picture.

54

Fairy Postboxes

Evie wants to post lots of letters to the fairies.
Can you match the sacks of letters to the right
fairy postboxes? Count the letters and draw lines
to the correct numbers.

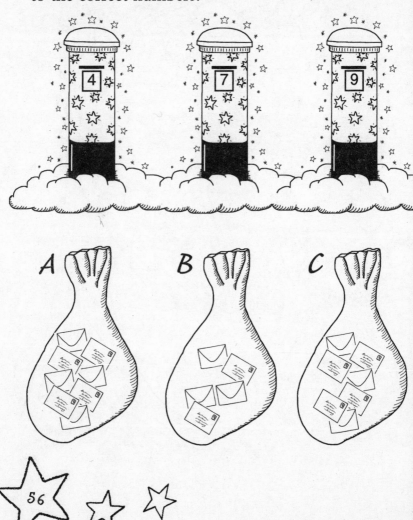

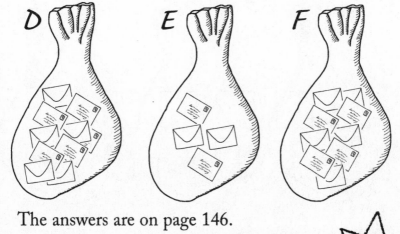

The answers are on page 146.

Get the Goodies

Oh no! Moonbeam's goody bag has got a hole in

58

it. She has dropped her gifts in the park on the way home from the fairy party.

Can you trace her path back and find the goodies?

Write how many you find in the boxes below.

The answers are on page 146.

Shadow Search

One of the fairy's spells has gone wrong and six fairies have lost their shadows.

Can you help them by drawing a line to the right shadow?

60

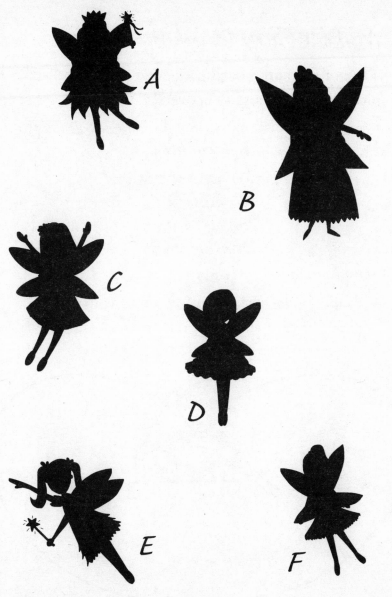

The answers are on page 147.

Make a Fairy Drinking Straw

These straws are fun to make and great for birthday parties and sleepovers!

You will need:

A piece of paper or thin card
Scissors
Pens for colouring
Drinking straws

How to make

1. Trace the fairy shape below on to your piece of paper or card and cut it out.

62

2. Colour in your fairy with your favourite colours.
3. Cut two slits in the fairy, on the dotted lines. (It helps to fold the fairy in half when you're doing this.)

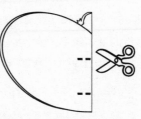

4. Insert the drinking straw, threading it through the two slits. Now you're ready for a fairy drink!

Fairy Tip If you're making a lot of straws for a party, why not personalize them with everyone's names? Or try different shapes, e.g. butterflies and stars.

63

Fairy Fun 2

What can you hear on a fairy's mobile phone?
A wing tone.

Why is Ruby the fairy like one of her favourite books?
They both like being red.

What's the difference between a fairy and a moth?
One likes to flutter by, the other's like a butterfly.

What kinds of stories do fairies tell cats?
Furry tales.

Knock, knock.
Who's there?
Fairy.
Fairy who?
Fairy nice to meet you!

Knock, knock.
Who's there?
Wing.
Wing who?
Wing me later, won't you?

Knock, knock.
Who's there?
Wand.
Wand who?
Wand to come to a party?

Flower Fun

Fairies love flowers, and this garden has three different kinds.

Count how many bluebells, tulips and roses there are growing and write the numbers below.

There are

_____

bluebells.

There are

_____

tulips.

There are

_____

roses.

The answers are on page 147.

67

Sky Crossword

Fairies love to fly around in the sky. What other things might you find up there?

CLUES

Across

2. It comes out a lot during the summer and it is very big, bright and hot.
3. We all live on Earth which, like Mars and Jupiter, is a ....
6. If you are lucky, you might see one of these colourful visions after a rainstorm. Perhaps you'll even find a crock of gold at the end of it!

Down

1. On a clear night you can see this in the sky. It might be full or crescent-shaped.
2. These twinkling things also come out at night. Some people like to make a wish upon them.
4. If it's raining, there's sure to be a few of these around.
5. You might see this zig-zag across the sky during a thunderstorm

The answers are on page 147.

69

Fairy Wordsnake

Below is a list of words associated with fairies. Can you trace the words in the grid opposite using a pencil? They go in one continuous line, snaking up and down, backwards and forwards, but never diagonally.

WINGS

WAND

SPELL

CHARM

FAIRYLAND

QUEEN

PALACE

CROWN

JEWELS

PETAL

MAGIC

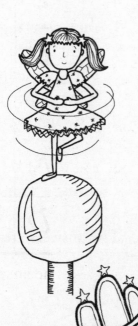

W	I	A	G	I	C
G	N	M	L	A	T
S	W	A	N	P	E
E	P	S	D	S	L
L	F	A	N	J	E
L	M	I	W	E	W
C	R	R	O	A	L
H	A	Y	R	C	A
N	A	L	C	E	P
D	Q	U	E	E	N

The answer is on page 147.

11

A Letter from the Fairies

The fairies have sent you a secret message – but it's in code!

Can you work out what they're saying by using the picture code below?

Write each letter in the space as you find it.

The answer is on page 148.

73

Cloud House Challenge

Dreamland is full of fairy cloud houses. Can you find six matching pairs?

Join the pairs with a pencil line.

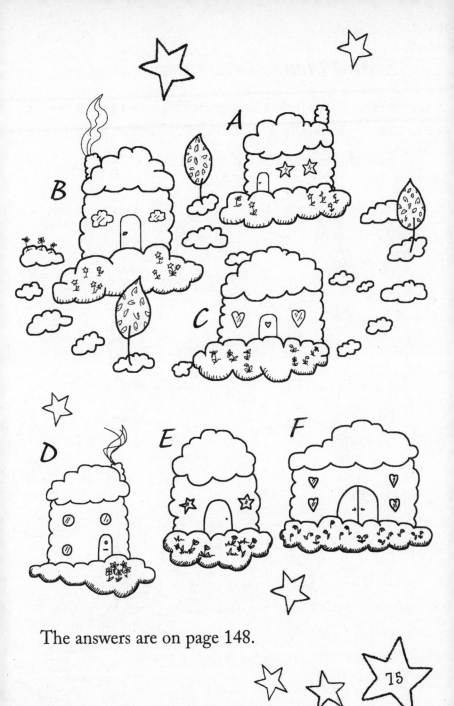

The answers are on page 148.

Star Maze

Evie must follow a star path through the night sky if she wants to reach Queen Celeste's palace.

But which path should she take?

The answer is on page 148.

77

Spot the Difference 1

Look closely at the two pictures below. They look similar, but there are ten differences in the second picture.

Can you circle the differences?

The answers are on page 148.

Tricky Toadstools

Can you complete these toadstool sums?

Draw the correct number of spots on each blank toadstool to finish the sum.

1

2

3

The answers are on page 148.

Tempting Toadstools

All fairies – and humans - will adore these yummy toadstools, made with marshmallows and the fairies' favourite – chocolate!

You will need:

A bag of marshmallows
A packet of round wine gums
A medium-sized bar of chocolate (white is best)
Smarties to decorate
Boiling water
Jugs/bowls
A grown-up to help!

How to make

1. Melt the chocolate – you will need a grown-up to help with this part as boiling water can be very dangerous. Ask your helper to boil a kettle and pour some water into a jug or fairly deep bowl. You will need to be able to rest a smaller bowl safely on top.

2. Break the chocolate up into small pieces and

put them into the smaller bowl. Place it on top of the jug of hot water and leave for five minutes, or until the chocolate is melted, stirring now and again.

3. When the chocolate is melted, dip the bottom of each wine gum into the chocolate and stick it to the bottom of a marshmallow.

4. Make as many 'toadstools' as you can and leave them on a plate until the chocolate has hardened. Putting them in a fridge or freezer for 5–10 minutes will speed this up.

5. Now take a cooled marshmallow and dip the top half into the melted chocolate. If the chocolate has hardened, ask a grown-up to help you melt it again. Decorate with three smarties.

6. Decorate all your toadstools and leave to cool.
   Toadstoolly delicious!

Mmm, these fairy toadstool treats are so tasty
you'll want to eat them all.

But don't forget to leave one out for the fairies!

Colour by Numbers

Fairies find petals very useful – this little fairy has used one as a sling for her arm.

Can you colour the picture using the numbers as your guide?

| 1. Pink | 3. Green | 5. Blue |
| 2. Yellow | 4. Brown | |

85

Wood Wordsearch

Woods and forests are good places to find fairies. But can you find eight other woodland things? The words may be up, down, across or diagonally, either forwards or backwards.

Draw a line through each word when you find it.

B	S	R	E	W	O	L	F	D	A
O	E	P	N	U	Q	E	M	L	N
G	L	T	R	E	E	J	O	E	H
K	E	C	A	D	Q	O	G	R	K
R	A	B	B	I	T	K	S	R	I
D	V	I	G	S	A	B	H	I	C
J	E	H	D	F	I	Q	B	U	A
O	S	A	E	R	L	I	M	Q	N
F	O	C	D	J	D	N	E	S	F
T	B	U	T	T	E	R	F	L	Y

Tree   Toadstool   Leaves
Butterfly   Flowers   Bird
Squirrel   Rabbit

The answers are on page 149.

Dot to Dot 2

Join the dots from 1 to 20 to find something associated with fairies.

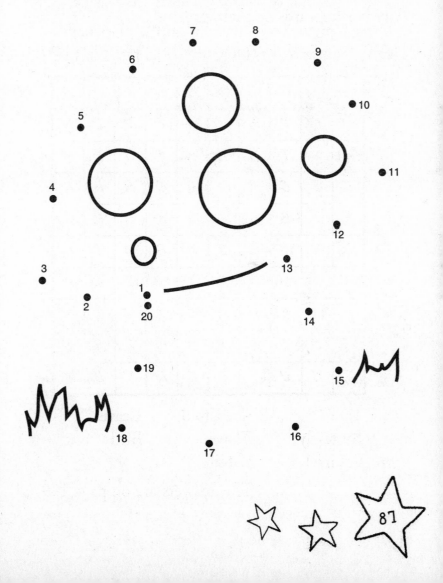

Simply Scrumptious

Mmm! The fairies certainly know how to make some delicious treats to eat.

Can you create a mouthwatering fairy snack?

Draw a picture of your treat on the plate below and give it a name. Here are some ideas to help you.

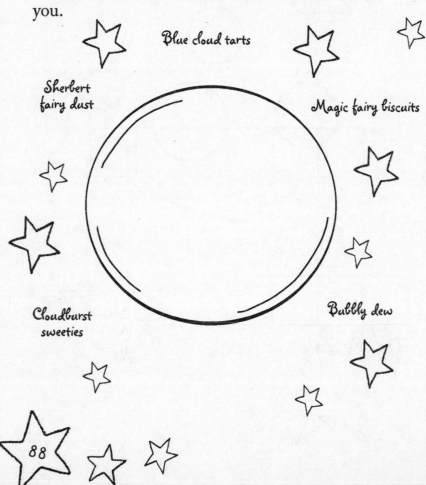

Blue cloud tarts

Sherbert fairy dust

Magic fairy biscuits

Cloudburst sweeties

Bubbly dew

Creature Feature

Some animals like to help fairies. Look at the picture clues below and write the names of the four friendly creatures in the grid.

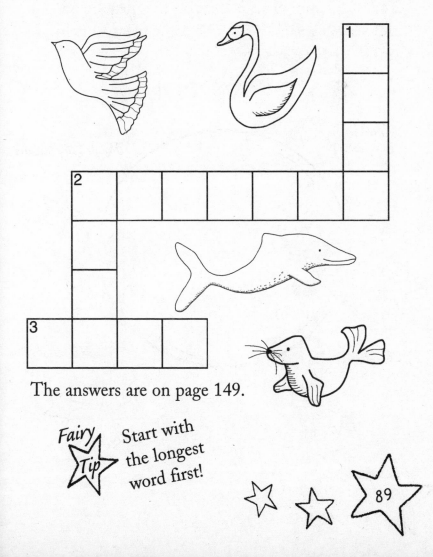

The answers are on page 149.

Fairy Tip Start with the longest word first!

Spot the Difference 2

There are four tooth fairies in each column, but only three of them are identical.

Can you spot the odd one out?

The answers are on page 149.

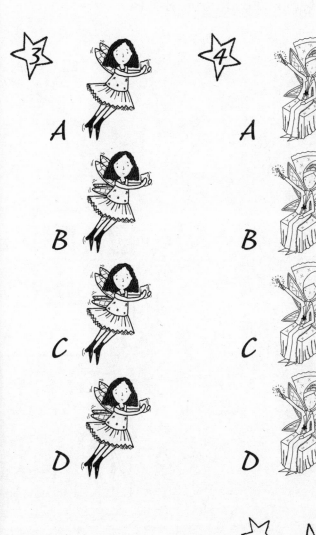

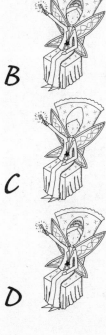

True or False?

The tooth fairies are out collecting teeth. Look carefully at this picture; then decide whether the statements opposite are true or false.

True or False? Tick the box.

1. There are five stars in the sky.
   True ☐ False ☐

2. One tooth fairy is sitting on a roof.
   True ☐ False ☐

3. A little boy has just been visited by a tooth fairy.
   True ☐ False ☐

4. There are no clouds in the sky.
   True ☐ False ☐

5. All the tooth fairies are flying.
   True ☐ False ☐

6. There are three lamp posts in the picture.
   True ☐ False ☐

The answers are on page 149.

93

Toothpaste Trail

Queen Eldora has lost her magic toothbrush wand. Can you find the right toothpaste trail to lead her to it?

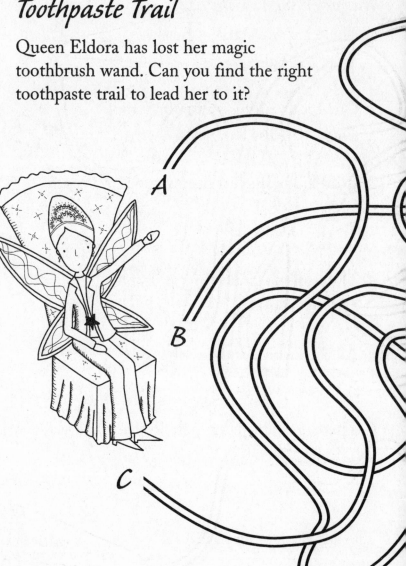

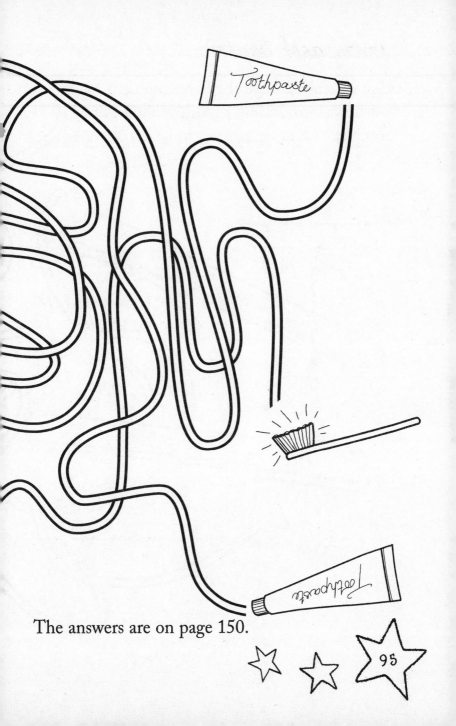

The answers are on page 150.

Toothbrush Teaser

Can you unscramble the letters on each magic toothbrush to find four tooth-related words?

Write the words in the spaces next to each brush.

1. _ _ _ _

2. _ _ _ _ _

3. _ _ _ _ _

4. _ _ _ _

The answers are on page 150.

Tumbling Teeth

Oh dear! That naughty tooth fairy Precious has been stealing teeth again.

In her rush to get away, she's dropped them all. Can you unscramble the teeth to find a person that the tooth fairies think you should visit now and again?

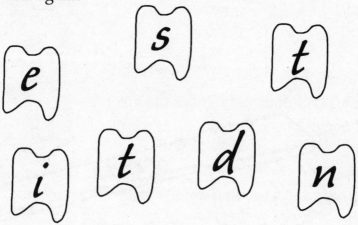

Write the letters in the correct order below:

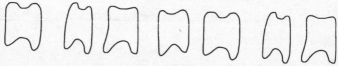

The answer is on page 150.

Tooth Fairy Fun

Why are tooth fairies like a pair of false teeth?
They both come out at night!

What is the tooth fairies' motto?
'The tooth, the whole tooth and nothing but the tooth.'

What do you call a boy who's just found money from the tooth fairy under his pillow?
A happy-gappy-chappy!

What's the best time for a wobbly tooth to come out?
Crunch time!

What do teeth like to do before they go to bed?
Read a bite-time story!

Make a Pop-up Fairy

Would you like to make a paper fairy that pops up to say hello? Here's how to do it!

You will need:
Three pieces of plain paper (A4 is best)
Scissors
Glue
Pens for colouring

How to make

1. Take two of your pieces of paper and fold them in half. On one of your folded pieces, make two cuts in the middle of the fold, like this:

Your cuts should be about 4 cm long and about 3 cm apart.

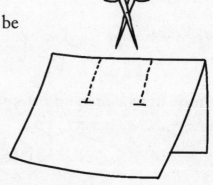

2. Unfold the two pieces of paper and stick them together. Put the glue round the *outside edge* of the paper, not in the middle (as this is the part that will pop up).

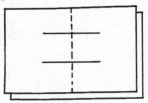

3. When the glue is dry, it's time for the clever bit (you may need a grown-up to help you). Stick your finger through the two slits in the middle and pull the fold out, like this:

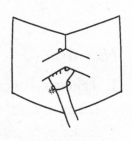

4. Fold the paper in half again and press it down, making sure that the slits are pressed outwards. When you open it up, you should have a box shape, like this:

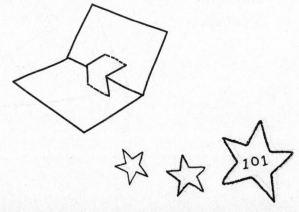

5. Trace the fairy template below on to your third piece of paper. Colour it in and cut it out carefully.

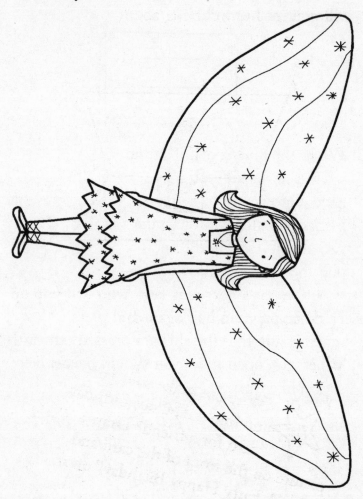

6. Stick the fairy on to the pop-up box. Position her carefully so that the main part of her body is firmly glued to the front of the box. This will prevent her wobbling about.

Now you've got a gorgeous fairy who will pop up every time you open up the card!

Fairy Tip Why not make your fairy pop up into a fabulous birthday card for a friend? Draw a picture on the front of the card and write 'A Fairy Happy Birthday!' on it.

Spot the Difference 3

Look carefully at these pictures of Eldora, the Tooth Fairy Queen. Can you spot six differences between them?

The answers are on page 150.

105

Moonlight Match

It's the middle of the night and the tooth fairies are flying off to visit all the children who have put a tooth under their pillow.

Can you match the silhouettes to the fairies on the opposite page?

The answers are on page 150.

Colouring Fun 2

Can you colour this picture of Queen Amethyst and a boy fairy using the guide below?

1. Purple
2. Green

3. Yellow
4. Brown

Fairy Tip Remember, Queen Amethyst's hair is snow white!

Cake Challenge

Mmm! Snowdrop's been baking some delicious fairy cakes. Can you spot which two cakes are exactly the same?

The answer is on page 151.

Fairy Food Fun

Find eight delicious treats that fairies love to eat! The words may be up, down, across or diagonally, either forwards or backwards.

Draw a line through each word when you find it.

B	A	U	G	N	I	C	I	H	B
I	E	M	D	W	F	A	J	S	E
S	W	E	E	T	S	I	W	T	F
C	O	L	W	S	E	K	A	C	S
U	M	N	A	H	Q	L	U	M	E
I	S	A	K	M	O	Y	D	U	I
T	U	B	I	C	P	N	U	A	R
S	C	H	O	A	F	U	E	T	R
I	A	H	O	J	A	S	W	Y	E
E	C	U	V	N	U	T	S	O	B

  Biscuits    Chocolate   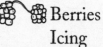 Berries
Cakes   Sweets   Icing
 Nuts   Honey

The answers are on page 151.

Fairy Bracelet

The fairies have started to make a beautiful flower bracelet.

Can you help them finish it by drawing your own flowers? Then you can colour it in.

Odd One Out 3

Look carefully at the pictures below. Can you circle the one picture in each column that is not the same as the first?

1

A

B

C

2

A

B

C

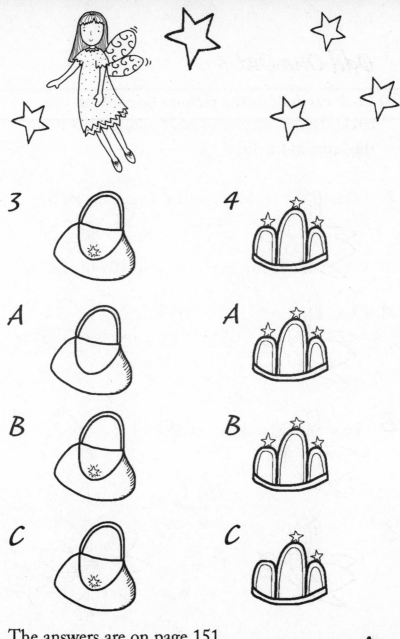

3

A

B

C

4

A

B

C

The answers are on page 151.

Fairy Fun 3

What do fairies brush their hair with?
Honey combs.

What is the fairies' favourite day of the week?
Flyday.

What's the tooth fairy's favourite day of the week?
Chewsday.

Where do fairies get their wands from?
Wanderland.

What do fairies do at school?
Spelling tests.

114

Dot to Dot 3

Join the dots to discover one of the fairies' favourite creatures.

Fairy Word Grid 2

Fill in the six words on the grid below by solving the clues opposite.

The first letter of each word will spell out a special gift that fairies sometimes give to lucky humans.

CLUES

1. Where fairies and toadstools can often be found.
2. What you can find on top of a fairy cake.
3. What a human must do before they can be small enough to visit Fairyland.
4. All fairies are proud of their beautiful, flowing
   ....
5. If you see a library book covered in sparkling fairy dust, chances are it's an .... book.
6. The name of a small white fairy and her special flower.

The answers are on page 151.

Make a Fairy Puppet

Here's how to make a puppet that you can use to perform in your own fairy show.

You will need:

A wooden spoon
Some pieces of wool
Poster paints and brushes
PVA glue
Scissors
A piece of paper
Ribbon/net/tissue to decorate

How to make

1. Paint a fairy face on the spoon. Give your fairy nice pink cheeks and perhaps a fringe (make sure it's the same colour as the wool you're using for the hair).

When the face is dry, paint the handle with a pretty pattern.

2. Make your fairy hair by cutting pieces of wool and tying them in the middle with another strand of wool.

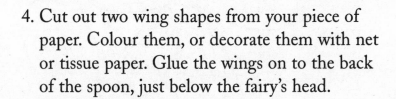

3. Glue the hair on to your spoon and add a decoration – ribbons, bows or perhaps one of your own hairclips or scrunchies?

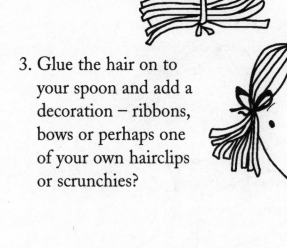

4. Cut out two wing shapes from your piece of paper. Colour them, or decorate them with net or tissue paper. Glue the wings on to the back of the spoon, just below the fairy's head.

5. Finally, use a piece of net or brightly coloured tissue paper to give your fairy a lovely skirt. Carefully scrunch up the top of the 'skirt' and glue it around the spoon. Now your fairy puppet is ready for her first performance!

Dot to Dot 4

Turn the page on its side and join the dots to find something that the Fairy Queen owns.

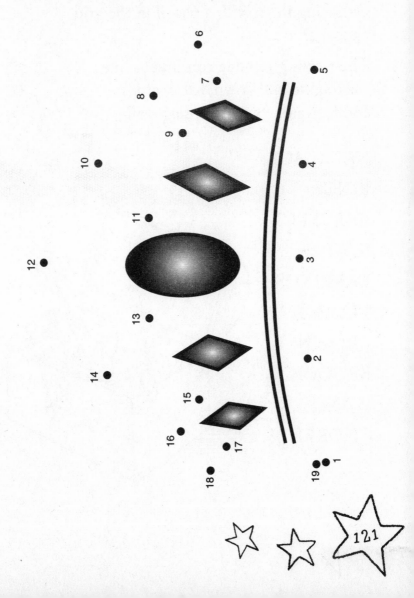

121

Treasure Wordsnake

We've discovered a hoard of glittering fairy treasure. Can you find the treasure words below by tracing them with a pencil in the grid opposite?

The words go in one continuous line, snaking up and down, backwards and forwards, but never diagonally.

NECKLACE

RING

BRACELET

JEWELS

EARRINGS

TIARA

CROWN

BROOCH

WAND

CHOKER

N	E	C	G	B	R
A	L	K	N	C	A
C	E	R	I	E	L
E	W	E	J	T	E
L	R	I	S	T	I
S	R	N	G	R	A
E	A	C	O	A	C
A	W	H	O	R	R
N	D	C	H	B	O
R	E	K	O	N	W

The answer is on page 152.

Count and Colour

It's the middle of the night and the tooth fairy Bonnie is visiting a little girl to collect her tooth. Let's hope that naughty Precious doesn't get there first!

How many of each of the objects below can you see in the picture?

Write the numbers then colour the picture in.

The answers are on page 152.

Fairy Colours

Read the clues below to identify the eight colours, then find the colours in the grid opposite. They are written across and down (not diagonally).

Why not use your favourite colour to shade in each word when you find it?

1. Queen Amethyst's favourite colour. It's also the colour of plums.
2. Fairy Ruby dresses in this colour.
3. The colour of daffodils.
4. Many book fairies have hair this colour – the colour of ink.
5. The colour of one of the fairies' favourite treats – chocolate.
6. The colour of royal crowns.
7. Snowdrop the fairy usually wears this colour.
8. Emerald the fairy's favourite colour.

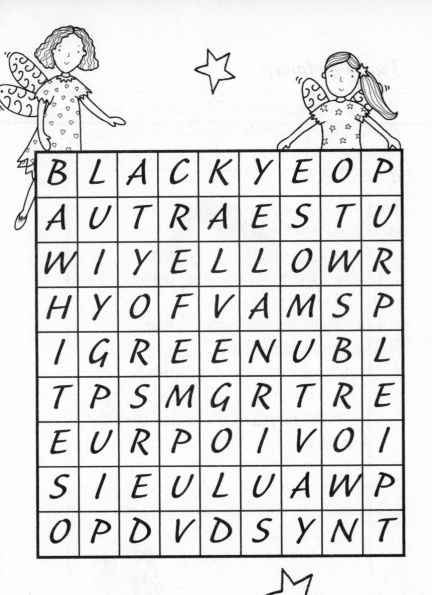

B	L	A	C	K	Y	E	O	P
A	U	T	R	A	E	S	T	U
W	I	Y	E	L	L	O	W	R
H	Y	O	F	V	A	M	S	P
I	G	R	E	E	N	U	B	L
T	P	S	M	G	R	T	R	E
E	U	R	P	O	I	V	O	I
S	I	E	U	L	U	A	W	P
O	P	D	V	D	S	Y	N	T

The answers are on page 152.

Double Trouble

Can you complete both fairy pictures by copying the missing parts from the picture opposite?

Then colour your fairy twins!

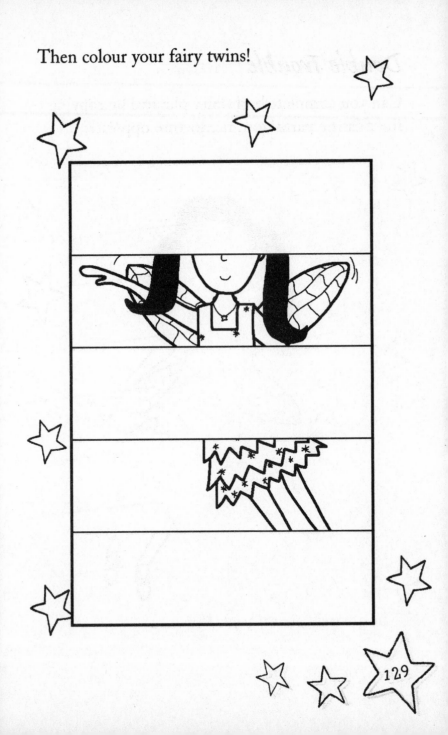

Dreamland Dilemma

Can you draw a line between the bed and the right duvet to make some dreamy words?

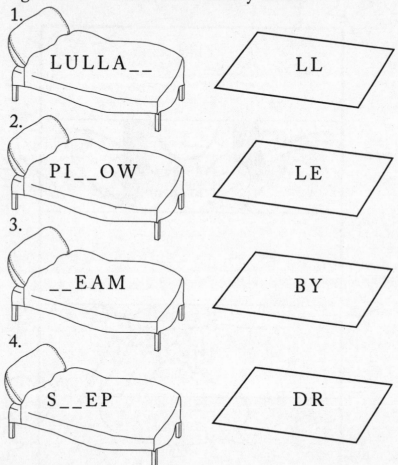

1. LULLA__   LL

2. PI__OW   LE

3. __EAM   BY

4. S__EP   DR

The answers are on page 153.

Shape Sorting

Can you read what each fairy is saying and match her to her favourite shape?

1. I like stars.

A.

2. Hearts are my favourite!

B.

3. Flowers are my thing.

C.

4. I just love moons!

D.

The answers are on page 153.

Make a Butterfly Brooch

Fairies love all kinds of jewellery and they also like butterflies. This lovely butterfly brooch is certainly fit for any fairy!

You will need:
A piece of thin card
Scissors
Glue and sticky tape
Small pieces of differently coloured tissue paper
Safety pin
Small beads (optional)

How to make

1. Copy or trace this butterfly shape on to your piece of card. Cut the shape out.

132

2. Take your tissue paper and use your card template to trace and cut out three or four butterfly shapes. Try to use a mix of different colours, if possible.

3. Put a small amount of glue on to the middle of the card shape (where the butterfly's body would be).

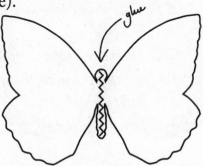

Stick on your first piece of tissue. Do the same again with the other pieces, sticking one on top of the other to create a lovely, layered effect.

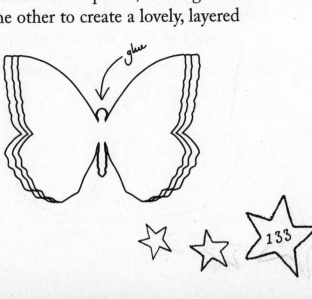

4. Now for the butterfly's body. You can either glue a line of small beads down the centre of the body, or use small balls of scrunched-up tissue paper instead (dark colours are best for the body).

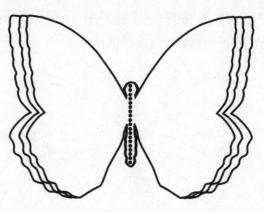

5. Finally, when your butterfly is dry, bend it slightly in half to create a 'flapping' effect. Use a small piece of sticky tape to stick the safety pin on the bend behind the butterfly.

And there you have it – a beautiful brooch that any fairy would be proud of!

Ring Maze

Ruby, Sapphire, Emerald and Connie are looking for the magical ruby ring that will help Ruby return to the fairy world.

Which of them will find the ring? Trace their paths on the maze to find out.

The answer is on page 153.

Name Search

Can you find the names of some of the characters from Gwyneth Rees's fairy books? The words may be up, down, across or diagonal, either forwards or backwards. Draw a line through each word when you find it.

S	N	O	W	D	R	O	P	L	O
O	W	S	U	S	T	A	R	I	T
M	I	E	B	T	I	K	C	M	P
R	W	V	K	O	H	S	A	H	W
U	D	I	U	L	K	E	F	E	L
B	H	E	P	A	B	I	B	I	O
Y	A	C	D	N	J	S	W	M	N
S	F	R	O	S	I	E	H	M	L
O	L	O	D	W	L	P	C	A	U
T	M	A	E	I	N	N	O	C	S

CONNIE   STAR

ROSIE   MOONBEAM

EVIE   SNOWDROP

CAMMIE   RUBY

The answers are on page 153.

Design a Duvet

Imagine having your own magical bed to transport you to Fairyland. What kind of duvet cover would it have?

Can you design a dreamy duvet cover for this magical bed?

How about using moons or stars, or perhaps flowers or hearts?

Fairy Rhymes

Can you complete each of these fairy rhymes with one word?

1. See the tiny fairies fly
   Up into the big blue _ _ _

2. Can this be a dream?
   The royal Fairy _ _ _ _ _

3. All the fairies like to eat
   Yummy snacks that taste so _ _ _ _ _

4. It's fun to mix and bake
   A delicious fairy _ _ _ _

5. This fairy's made a mess
   All down her pretty _ _ _ _ _

6. Oh, wouldn't it be grand
   To visit Fairy_ _ _ _ _

The answers are on page 153.

Are You a Fairy Fan?

Gwyneth Rees writes fantastic stories about fairies and the girls who meet them. How much do you know about the fairy world in Gwyneth's books?

Find out in our fun quiz!

1. What is the fairies' favourite thing to eat?

2. What do the tooth fairies use as wands?

3. In Dreamland, what are the fairies' houses made from?

4. In the book *Fairy Dust*, Rosie makes friends with a small male fairy (known as a 'wee man'). Can you remember his name?

5. A book fairy enters our world through a special magic book in a library. What is the book called?

6. What do fairies sprinkle when they do a magic spell?

7. In the book *Fairy Treasure*, Ruby the fairy can't go back to Fairyland unless she finds something that she once lost. What is it?

8. How would you get a letter to Queen Celeste, in Fairyland?

9. Which bird do fairies sometimes ride on?

10. Can you name four of Gwyneth Rees's fairies?

The answers are on page 154.

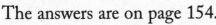

Answers

page 6 – Odd One Out 1
Fairie's 3, 4, 7 and 14 are the odd ones out.

page 8 – Dolphin Dilemma
B

page 10 – Fairy Crossword
Across

1. wings	2. queen	3. dust
5. library	6. chocolate	

Down

1. wand	4. sparkle

page 12 – Fairy Clothes Match
The boot has no double.

page 16 – Magical Mix-up

1. kind	2. tiny	3. helpful
4. pretty	5. sweet	

page 20 – Find Cammie's Sock
C

143

page 21 – Fairy Favourites
1. chocolate   2. wands   3. picnics
4. music   5. shoes   6. parties

page 24 – Puzzling Piles
D

page 26 – Find the Fairies
There are 12 fairies hiding.

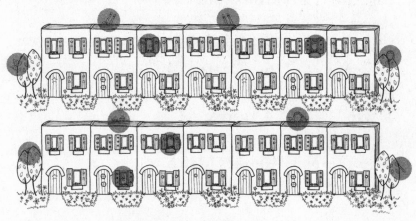

page 28 – Biscuit Blunder
1. Emerald   2. Ruby   3. Sapphire

page 30 – Pick the Page:
1 – A, 2 – D, 3 – B, 4 – E, 5 – C, 6 – F

page 38 – Flower Wordsnake

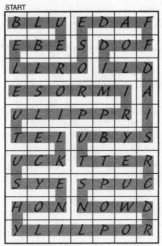

START

B	L	U	E	D	A	F
E	B	E	S	D	O	F
L	L	R	O	I	L	D
E	S	O	R	M	I	A
U	L	I	P	P	R	I
T	E	L	U	B	Y	S
U	C	K	T	T	E	R
S	Y	E	S	P	U	C
H	O	N	N	O	W	D
Y	L	I	L	P	O	R

page 41 – Odd One Out 2
Bunch D is the odd one out.

page 42 – Puzzling Palaces

145

page 44 – Where's the wand?

page 46 – Party Shopping
1. invitations   2. lemonade   3. biscuits
4. straws   5. chocolate muffins
6. crisps

page 50 – Fairy Word Grid 1
1. party   2. envelope   3. twinkle
4. apples   5. lantern
Word spelled: petal

page 56 – Fairy Postboxes
4 – E, 7 – C, 9 – F, 5 – B, 8 – A, 10 – D

page 58 – Get the Goodies

1	3	2	8	3

page 60 – Shadow Search
1 – F, 2 – A, 3 – C, 4 – E, 5 – D, 6 – B

page 66 – Flower Fun
9 bluebells, 4 tulips, 8 roses.

page 68 – Sky Crossword
Across
2. sun   3. planet
6. rainbow
Down
1. moon   2. stars
4. clouds   5. lightning

page 70 – Fairy Wordsnake

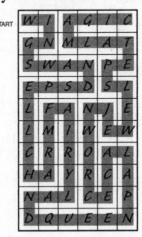

page 72 – A Letter from the Fairies
The message reads: Keep looking and one day
you might see us!

page 74 – Cloud House Challenge
1 – E, 2 – F, 3 – D, 4 – A, 5 – B, 6 – C

page 76 – Star Maze
Evie should take path 1.

page 78 – Spot the Difference 1

page 80 – Tricky Toadstools

1. $4 + 2 = 6$	2. $3 + 5 = 8$	3. $5 + 4 = 9$
4. $6 - 2 = 4$	5. $8 - 2 = 6$	6. $2 \times 4 = 8$
7. $3 \times 3 = 9$		

page 86 – Wood Wordsearch

B	S	R	E	W	O	L	F	D	A
O	E	P	N	U	Q	E	M	L	N
G	L	T	R	E	E	J	O	E	H
K	E	C	A	D	Q	O	G	R	K
R	A	B	B	I	T	K	S	R	I
D	V	I	G	S	A	B	H	I	C
J	E	H	D	F	I	Q	B	U	A
O	S	A	E	R	L	I	M	Q	N
F	O	C	D	J	D	N	E	S	F
T	B	U	T	T	E	R	F	L	Y

page 89 – Creature Feature
1. swan   2 (across). dolphin
2 (down). dove 3. seal

page 90 – Spot the Difference 2
1 – D, 2 – B, 3 – A, 4 – C

page 93 – True or False?
1. False – there are 9   2. True
3. False – it's a girl   4. True
5. False   6. False – there are 4

149

page 94 – Toothpaste Trail
Queen Eldora should take toothpaste trail B.

page 96 – Toothbrush Teaser
1. gums   2. brush
3. mouth   4. bite

page 98 – Tumbling Teeth
The word spelled out by the teeth is: dentist

page 104 – Spot the Difference 3

page 106 – Moonlight Match
1 – D, 2 – E, 3 – A, 4 – C, 5 – B

page 109 – Cake Challenge
Cakes 1 and 8 are the same.

page 110 – Fairy Food Fun

B	A	U	G	N	I	C	I	H	B
I	E	M	D	W	F	A	J	S	E
S	W	E	E	T	S	I	W	T	F
C	O	L	W	S	E	K	A	C	S
U	M	N	A	H	Q	L	U	M	E
I	S	A	K	M	O	Y	D	U	I
T	U	B	I	C	P	N	U	A	R
S	C	H	O	A	F	U	E	T	R
I	A	H	O	J	A	S	W	Y	E
E	C	U	V	N	U	T	S	O	B

page 112 – Odd One Out 3
1 – B, 2 – B, 3 – A, 4 – C

page 116 – Fairy Word Grid 2
1. woods   2. icing
3. shrink   4. hair
5. entry   6. snowdrop
word spelled: wishes

151

page 122 – Treasure Wordsnake

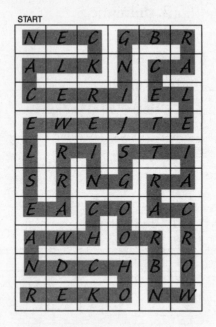

page 124 – Count and Colour

1 lamp	9 books	2 fairies
4 socks	7 pencils	3 wands

page 126 – Fairy Colours

1. purple   2. red
3. yellow   4. black
5. brown   6. gold
7. white   8. green

152

page 130 – Dreamland Dilemma
1. lullaby   2. pillow
3. dream   4. sleep

page 131 – Shape Sorting
1 – A, 2 – D, 3 – B, 4 – C

page 135 – Ring Maze
Emerald finds the ring.

page 136 – Name Search

S	N	O	W	D	R	O	P	L	O
O	W	S	U	S	T	A	R	I	T
M	I	E	B	T	I	K	C	M	P
R	W	V	K	O	H	S	A	H	W
U	D	I	U	L	K	E	F	E	L
B	H	E	P	A	B	I	B	I	O
Y	A	C	D	N	J	S	W	M	N
S	F	R	O	S	I	E	H	M	L
O	L	O	D	W	L	P	C	A	U
T	M	A	E	I	N	N	O	C	S

page 138 – Fairy Rhymes
1. sky   2. Queen   3. sweet
4. cake   5. dress   6. land

page 140 – Are You a Fairy Fan?

1. chocolate
2. magic toothbrushes
3. clouds
4. Cammie
5. an entry book
6. fairy dust
7. a ruby ring
8. post it in a fairy postbox
9. swans
10. any four of:

Snowdrop	Cammie the wee man
Queen Mae	Ruby
Emerald	Sapphire
Queen	Amethyst
Moonbeam	Star
Queen Celeste	Twinkle
Sky	Buttercup
Bonnie	Goldie
Queen Eldora	Precious

Gwyneth Rees

fairy dust

*When Rosie finds a tiny tartan sock in her bedroom,
she's sure it could only fit one thing – a fairy!
Mum tells Rosie not to be so silly, fairies don't exist.*

Then the old lady who lives next door tells Rosie that
Mum's the one who's silly, fairies are everywhere if you
know how to look. And they love chocolate.

Rosie's not sure who to believe until she sees something in the grass at the top of the moor and then she
can hardly believe her eyes.

Could it really be a fairy . . . ?

Gwyneth Rees

fairy treasure

Connie has never believed in fairies, so she is amazed when Ruby, a tiny fairy-girl, suddenly appears in the library of the old house where Connie is staying.

Ruby says that she is a book fairy – but that she is in terrible trouble. She has been banished from fairyland until she finds a ruby ring which she has lost.

Can Connie help Ruby find the missing ring – before the doorway to fairyland is closed forever?

Evie had always believed in fairies,
but she has never seen one . . .

When Grandma is taken into hospital, Evie finds herself sleeping in Grandma's old brass bed – and being
visited by Moonbeam and Star, two dream fairies
who whisk her away on a magical journey to Queen
Celeste's palace in fairyland.

Moonbeam and Star tell Evie they can't make Grandma
better, but they can give her a wonderful adventure so
long as she is sleeping in a magic bed. Can Evie find
a way to make Grandma's fairy dreams come true?

Gwyneth Rees

fairy gold

Lucy can't believe her eyes when she wakes one night to find two fairies in her little sister's bedroom.

The fairies tell Lucy that their names are Goldie and Bonnie – and they are tooth fairies. Their special job is to collect children's teeth and make a spell that creates golden Goodness.

But there is trouble in fairyland. A selfish fairy wants all the Goodness for herself. With the help of the Tooth Fairy Queen, can Lucy and her new friends stop the thieving fairy – before the gold has all gone?

There's a secret world at the bottom of the sea!

Rani came to Tingle Reef when she was a baby mermaid – she was found fast asleep in a seashell, and nobody knows where she came from.

Now strange things keep happening to her – almost as if by magic. What's going on? Rani's pet sea horse, Roscoe, Octavius the octopus and a scary sea-witch help her find out . . .

'A-A-A-TISHOO!'
Cosmo burst out, sending a huge shower of magic sneeze into the cauldron.

Cosmo has always wanted to be a witch-cat, just like his father, so when he passes the special test he's really excited. Now he can use his magic sneeze to help Sybil the witch mix her spells.

Sybil is very scary and no one trusts her. But when she starts brewing a top-secret spell recipe, Cosmo begins to worry. Could Sybil be cooking up a truly terrifying potion? And could the special ingredients be KITTENS?

A selected list of titles available from Macmillan Children's Books

The prices shown below are correct at the time of going to press.
However, Macmillan Publishers reserves the right to show new retail prices
on covers, which may differ from those previously advertised.

Gwyneth Rees

Fairy Dust	ISBN-13: 978-0-330-41554-5	£4.99
	ISBN-10: 0-330-41554-9	
Fairy Treasure	ISBN-13: 978-0-330-43730-1	£4.99
	ISBN-10: 0-330-43730-5	
Fairy Dreams	ISBN-13: 978-0-330-43476-8	£4.99
	ISBN-10: 0-330-43476-4	
Fairy Gold	ISBN-13: 978-0-330-43938-1	£4.99
	ISBN-10: 0-330-43938-0	
Mermaid Magic	ISBN-13: 978-0-330-42632-9	£4.99
	ISBN-10: 0-33-42632-X	
Cosmo and the Magic Sneeze	ISBN-13: 978-0-330-43729-5	£4.99
	ISBN-10: 0-330-43729-1	

All Pan Macmillan titles can be ordered from our website,
www.panmacmillan.com, or from your local bookshop
and are also available by post from:

Bookpost, PO Box 29, Douglas, Isle of Man IM99 1BQ
Credit cards accepted. For details:
Telephone: 01624 677237
Fax: 01624 670923
Email: bookshop@enterprise.net
www.bookpost.co.uk

Free postage and packing in the United Kingdom